BINARY JAZZ

SHAUN O. McCOY

SISYPHEAN PUBLISHING

This is a work of fiction. The personalities contained within, both artificial and biological, are fictitious, and any similarities between them and any actual personalities are strictly coincidental.

Binary Jazz

Edited by: Leigh Thomas

Title art: Thomas the Younger
Title Layout: Michael Cannon

A Sisyphean Publishing Book

ISBN-13: 978-0615990989 (Sisyphean Publishing)
ISBN-10: 0615990983

First Edition March 2014

Printed in the United States of America

0 9 8 7 6 5 4

PRAISE FOR SHAUN O. MCCOY AND BINARY JAZZ

"Finally, a robot I can get behind!"
—*Thomas the Younger, Author of These Windows*

"A robot that speaks to the human condition."
— *Matt Michaelis, Author of the Kids Summon series*

"I read McCoy and enjoy him. If you have an ounce of imagination, so will you. He takes you places you can't go by yourself."
—*McKendree Long, Author of Dog Soldier Moon*

"I could read about McCoy's robot butler again and again."
—*Laura Valtorte, Filmmaker, Author of Family Meal*

"[McCoy] writes with a passion, layering emotion on fantasy and science fiction, drawing in readers from beyond his genre."
—*Ginny Padgett, President of SCWW*

"McCoy is a talented and bright young writer."
—*B. Butler, Author of Murder in Cairo*

[McCoy's] characters are soulful, . . . surprising us with their humanity and evoking our laughter in unexpected ways."
—*Chris Mathews, Author of GARGOYLES*

OTHER WORKS BY SHAUN O. MCCOY

For Leigh Thomas

ACKNOWLEDGEMENTS

I had never intended to write another Arty story.

The people who should be acknowledge here are the ones who wrote emails, reviews, and Facebook messages (or in some cases, all three) requesting for a sequel to *Electric Blues* (aka *eBlues*). It is because of you that I have written this story.

I should also mention Monet Jones, a colleague of mine and a brilliant author, who was the first person to suggest the Arty adventures continue all the way back when *eBlues* was just a short story published in MBrane SF.

BINARY JAZZ

Percentage Occurrences of a Ham and Cheese Sandwich in Gil's Lunch Bag Delineated by Month

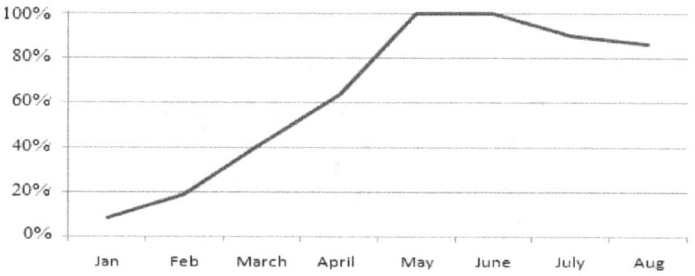

1001001101000010011101010111010000100000011100101101111011101011001001001110110110011001000100100000110100001100100101100 0010111001001100100001000000111010001101000011010001001000001100101011110000110000101100001011101000091000000411001101 1011111011011100110011001100100000011000100011001010110011001101111011101100110010001001001110101010100000011010000101010010 10100111101100110001000000110001101101101111011101010111001000001011100101001001011000100000100000001100000011011101 050001001001001000000110011001001101011111011101011101010104101010101111001010011010110011110011011110110011001001010110 11011110100100000119101101100101011001010110000010000011011101110000111110001101001000110010101000010101100100010100 1001101111011110011001001101101011011000011110100110100101101011101110110111000010000001101010011011000101101001011001001 0010000110110101100100101010110101011011011111011110111001001111001001001000110010110111100001000000110011011011000010111000 0000011000110010001110101011011011110010000001110100010100011001010010010011001001100101011001011100001010110111011001100

An alcoholic is never cured, I'm told, no matter how long they stay sober. I cannot drink, so I cannot be an alcoholic—but perhaps depression is the same way. They say no matter how far it has sunk behind a person, it is always lurking—waiting—biding its time until the circumstances are right . . . and then . . .

I'm Arty, PA3025, and I struggle with Artificial Initiative and Agency Syndrome. I have a job. I work from 9am to 5pm at Vespasian Research doing routine maintenance on second stage xenon based refrigeration units. I have a domestic. Her name is Decker. She depends on me. I have two friends, Knickers and Gil. And I have purpose, or at least I feel like I do—so long as I take one day at a time.

[U+2029]

"Jesus Christ, Arty," Gil said, "you sound like a goddamn self-help book."

Gil is my friend, so I know I am not supposed to report him to Human Resources for his breach of language conduct. I have noticed that his use of taboo words is highly correlated with the cafeteria, accounting for 70% of all observed instances.

"That is very perceptive," I told him. "I have been researching different therapy techniques in hopes that they will have analogous applications to my own problem sets."

He took a bite out of his ham and cheese sandwich. Gil is the kind of human being who leaves his mouth ajar while chewing. Originally, I thought this action might carry a connotation of disrespect as I have read several sources which state that such behavior is rude. However, I have noticed that rigid cultural protocols bother Gil, and I have hypothesized that his uncouth behavior is actually indicative of his wish to share an informal relationship.

"I've been looking into some of that too," he said around his food. "Well, not like yesterday, but after Ruth left, I thought . . ." he swallowed. "Well I thought maybe I could use some help, man, you know? I mean, a *divorce*. That's a lot for anybody. Not that I thought she left because I was messed up. I just thought that it might be smart."

"I think that was very pragmatic research to do, Gil."

Gil had reported his and Ruth's relationship difficulties when I had first met him in January of this year. On April 14th he advised me that she had left their domicile and that they were legally separated. When two machines have difficulty communicating, they erase their current material/information transfer protocols out of their function sets and replace them with protocols agreed to by both parties. Humans cannot rewrite their material/information transfer protocols, so they instead seek out a third party for arbitration. In humans this is more exciting because they often do not follow their assigned protocols. Ruth was doing this now by seeing a man named Chuck. Chuck works as a corporate defense lawyer.

"Sometimes I don't get her, you know?" Gil was now eating sea salt and vinegar potato chips. "She does things just to be rude. I mean, she left *me*. I'm the one who's supposed to be mean."

"I have noticed that you rarely act negatively towards others, except the snack machine."

I had written several programs for myself about humor. The essence of humor, as best I have been able to devise, is found either in unexpected failure or the incorrect attribution of one idea to another. I often make the latter as a mistake naturally, so I thought it should be easy for me to use a compilation of these errors as a data set to inform my humor protocols. Gil did not laugh, however. My current success rate with humor is below 30%. Knickers tells me not to try. He says I am naturally funny.

"I think that's the problem with me, Arty. She thinks I'm *too* nice. You know what I told her?"

"I do not."

He looked confused. "You don't what?"

"I do not know what reply you made to Ruth."

His chip bag crinkled as he took out another selection

of chips. "Oh, right. I told her it was because she was too mean. Seriously, Arty. Sometimes she treats me like Richard treats you, you know? Like she thinks I'm less than a person."

"You believe that Richard thinks I am less than a person?" I asked.

"I don't know. But too *nice,* Arty? Too *nice!* Does that even make sense?"

"I do not know. I understand why you find the comment counter-intuitive. I will run a game theory analysis to see if her complaint might have any basis in—"

Gil raised his hand and shook his head. "Maybe you're right, Arty. I think she went with me because she thought I had a bit of an edge, you know. Girls like that. Guys with an edge. 'Cause I'm a maintenance guy, I used to get those kind of girls a lot. I should have been meaner to her, you know . . . less of a pushover. I tried that last night, being mean."

This seemed unwise. "I think now is probably not the time to be mean to Ruth. I would not estimate your probability of being able to resolve your relationship differences as being very high, and it seems to me like causing her further emotional aggravation . . ."

He laughed. This was unexpected. I would have to run this conversation back again later when I had more power to allocate to my processor. I was unable to determine why he had not laughed at my joke about the snack machine, but had instead found my last statement funny.

Gil held up the chip bag and poured the last of the

chips into his mouth. I admired this about Gil. He was often very efficient, not just in his calorie consumption, but in his work in general.

He chewed the chips and swallowed. "I wouldn't mind causing her some emotional aggravation. But I don't want her back, Arty. I was talking about being mean to a different girl. A girl I didn't know."

I was confused. "Why would you want to cause emotional aggravation to someone you didn't know?" I had not noted Gil as having sadistic tendencies, but Knickers had warned me that situations of distress often changed people's behavior patterns.

"I was out at the Speakeasy last night, the bar on 112th. I'm telling you, that mean thing was working for me."

"In aggravating the woman?"

"In the way that women like to be aggravated, Arty."

"I see. You were flirting with her."

"Now you're talking my language! Only it's pretty hard for a guy to pick up a girl when he's out on his own. Now if I was back in Denver, I'd have plenty of friends I could go out to the bars with, you know? Since I moved here to be with Ruth, though, I hadn't been out making those kinds of friends. Those aren't the guys a married man wants to be with."

He was likely correct in this. I had witnessed many humans of both genders expressing dissatisfaction with their mate's alcohol consumption. "It is very likely that the wrong peer group would have had an adverse effect on your relationship with Ruth."

"I'll say." He opened his soda can.

Gil was efficient in this way, too. He rarely started to consume liquids before he had finished the solid portions of his meal, and he always imbibed them rather quickly.

"I wish I'd had someone out with me at the Speakeasy. It's easier to talk to the ladies, you know, when you're with someone."

"Why is that?"

"Well, maybe because there's more than one of them. Maybe because all the attention isn't on me, you know. It just is."

I had no reason to doubt his claim.

He sipped his soda in silence for a moment. I considered a variety of things that had happened to me today as possible conversation topics. This wasn't usually necessary with Gil, as he seldom required a stimulus point from which to talk. Knickers was very right about those behavioral changes.

"Even if you don't get a girl," he said, "it's nice to be out with another person, you know?"

He was silent for another few moments, looking at me as if he was expecting me to say something.

Decker had been particularly loud this morning. I was thinking about taking her to the veterinarian. However, her mewling, though given at a higher rate and with higher decibels than usual, was still below the threshold I had assigned as being likely symptomatic of a health issue. However, if she continued to show signs of distress when I got home from work this evening, it would put her recent cumulative average over that threshold.

"It was a great club," Gil told me. "Even had a Jazz band playing. You listen to music, Arty?"

"I do not."

"Not at all?"

"I have downloaded songs before in order to analyze their aesthetic, but I have not found any reason to listen to them in real time."

"Well why don't you come out this weekend. Check it out. It's more, how would you say it, *variable* when it's live. Do you have any plans on Friday night?"

"I do not."

"Well great!" he said. "I'll take the car to work, and we can go there after our shift ends."

He did not appear to be asking my permission, but I thought I would let him know that his plan was acceptable to me. "I will mark it in my calendar."

I liked this statement because it was both literally true and conveyed the correct information to the people I was making plans with. I had learned to say it from listening to Knickers.

"Alright!" Gil's face showed signs that he was pleased. "Great. You and me versus the world, Arty."

[U+2029]

I had not gone out with a human being for a social occasion before, so I thought I would speak to Knickers in order to get his advice. I sent him an email asking to meet before Friday. I was a Personal Assistant, so I still like to use email. Knickers says continued email use is symptomatic of me being old fashioned as there is no reason I couldn't send my requests through social networking mediums. He says that I picked this up from working with Madeline Albright, though I believe he is mistaken. I think I am old fashioned because I am obsolete.

I arrived at Knickers' apartment after work on Tuesday.

His apartment is on the second floor. An enterprising weed was growing out of a crack at the base of his concrete steps. I was careful not to disturb it on my way up. Knickers was working when I arrived. I waited patiently for him to finish. After two minutes and a few seconds he swiveled his chair around and rolled up to his desk.

He was drinking bottled water today, and he was well shaved. In general, these were signs that Knickers was doing well.

He smiled. "You know, you are officially cured of your AIAS, Arty. And even if you weren't, you're not on welfare, so you don't have to keep sending me reports of all your downloads."

"I am aware of this, Knickers, but you are part of my network. You often send me kitten subject matter videos, so I thought I would reciprocate."

Knickers' grin grew wider. "Did you see the one where

the kitten was skateboarding?"

"I did, Knickers."

"I bet you Decker couldn't do that!"

"I believe you are correct in that assumption, Knickers."

He leaned forward and picked up his water bottle. He idly fiddled with the cap, unscrewing it and rescrewing it without actually opening the bottle completely. "Well, since it's cool that I'm looking at all of your downloads, what's up with all this material on dating?"

Knickers knows me very well.

"That is actually what I had hoped to discuss with you," I told him. "Gil, my co-worker, has invited me out to a bar. I think he intends to find a replacement mate while he's there."

"Excellent, Arty!" Knickers said. "I'm always glad to hear it when you make friends—but, uh, what did you mean when you said 'replacement mate'?"

"Gil is going through a divorce."

"Huh. Poor guy. Do you know where you guys are going?"

"I do. It is Speakeasy, on 112th Street. I have looked up the band that is scheduled to play there and downloaded their recorded music."

"Did you like it?"

I was not sure how to answer the question. "They play jazz music. The quality of the recording is poor."

"Well that'll be fixed when you hear it live. You know what might be fun, Arty? Is if you try and guess which note is going to come next."

"I have downloaded their songs, Knickers. I do not know that it will be difficult to determine the upcoming notes."

He unscrewed the bottle cap completely and took a sip of his water. "Well, I think you'll find jazz is a little less . . . scripted . . . than you're used to. Oh, and there's a song I love. Honeysuckle Rose. Request, it, will you?"

I would not enjoy the song, but I determined that I would request to hear it anyway. Like the cat subject matter videos, it could serve as a talking point.

"So the dating material you've been reading is so you can be a good wingman?"

"That term accurately describes the role I will attempt to fill. It seems like an odd request to make of an AI, though."

"Maybe," Knickers said, "but in a way, you might be uniquely suited for this job."

"How so?"

"Well, you're not likely to steal away the man's replacement mate, are you?"

This seemed like an appropriate time to try for some humor. "Not unless he falls for a toaster."

Knickers laughed.

I'm still under 30%, but I'm getting closer.

[U+0085]

Gil's Cursing Occurrences by Location

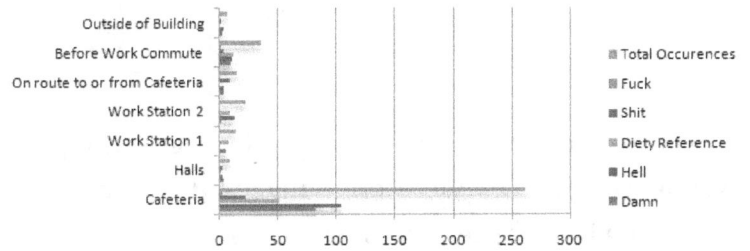

- 1 -

The rest of the week passed fairly uneventfully. My experiences at work were normative and whatever had been ailing Decker seemed to have passed.

After having read and processed 2GB worth of information on human dating practices, I considered myself well prepared for the upcoming evening in an academic sense. Much of the information I'd downloaded wasn't applicable to me. There was little I could do to make sure Gil was in a stable, self-actualized place. There was also a troubling, though prevalent, opinion held by many authors which stated that a person was most likely to find a mate while they were not actively searching for one. I found this troubling, since if true, this meant our objective was doomed to failure simply because we were attempting it. However, I noticed this advice came primarily from people who lacked the relevant credentials in psychology. For the success of our evening, I could only hope that those who espoused it did so only because they were bad at finding a mate.

My other worry was the amount of power I was consuming. I was having to exhaust more of my battery than usual because of Richard.

Richard is one of the many workers who runs

maintenance checks on the refrigeration units during the shift before I arrive. Many of our machines overlap. When he knows that I will be the next worker to service them (whether later that day for x900s or on the day after for the x800s) he tends to employ practices which inhibit my efficiency. For example, he often misplaces the keys to open the maintenance panels. One of his habits is to leave the graphene filters exposed to the air so I have to purge them before they can detect xenon purity. Unfortunately there are no company policies against these practices, so I have nothing to cite him for. I find his behavior very disturbing because he does not exhibit it towards other workers. I can only assume, therefore, that his actions must be directed towards me, and that they most probably carry malicious intent.

Normally, the amount of units which we both work on is rather small, however today I have found that over 50% of them have undergone Richard's sabotage. Since the machines were usually assigned in blocks at random from the Vespasian server, such a high percentage of overlap is extremely unlikely. At first I considered the possibility that Richard may have deliberately swapped some of his units with other workers in order to cause me more harm, however, it seemed unlikely that Richard disliked me that much so I dismissed the fear as being paranoid.

Even so, I composed an email to Ben Greer, my immediate report, requesting company policy be changed so as to make the graphene tampering a citable offence. I gave him the statistics of the high percentage occurrences I had today. I considered mentioning Richard as a culprit, but this seemed excessive. If Ben Greer consented to my request, Richard would no longer be able to harm me in this way.

Right after I sent the email, Gil stopped and spoke to me. "You ready for tonight?"

"I may have to ask that we delay our departure for some time. I have had trouble keeping up with my expected work load today."

Gil's eyes narrowed with confusion. "You? Having trouble?"

"Richard has left the graphene filters exposed in my units, and he has done so today in over half of them."

"What a douche-spigot." Gil seemed genuinely concerned.

I was going to have to add another category to Gil's breaches in language protocol. "Indeed, his behavior is most unbecoming."

"You should talk to Greer about this. That ain't right. It's like the guy is out to get you or something."

I noted Gil's opinion. "Perhaps. However, I have asked for a change in protocol with Ben Greer. It is my hope that this measure will be sufficient. If it is not, I will consider more drastic measures."

Gil patted me on the shoulder. "Well, hey man, I'm a little ahead of schedule. If you want to pass me a few of your units I'd be glad to help out."

I made a quick cost-benefit analysis. "That would be an efficient use of our labor resource."

He grinned. "It would indeed."

It is good, I am learning, to have friends.

[U+2029]

Humans sweat, so it is inadvisable for them to wear high end clothes in a work environment. Gil had circumvented this problem by bringing an extra shirt with him. He was wearing the shirt as I approached his automobile.

Since much of the advice I had read about human dating interaction was centered around Gil's self-actualization, I had decided to pay him a compliment. "I believe that your perspective mates will be comfortable with your aesthetic choice."

He smiled. "Why thank you, Arty. You aren't looking bad yourself."

His vehicle was old enough to have a driver's seat. I remembered that Ruth was taking their more modern vehicle.

Gil sat in the back seat next to me. "Speakeasy, 112th."

The windshield lit up with directions and a picture of the establishment in question. "Is this your desired location?" the car asked.

"Sure is, Gretel."

Decker seemed to be lonely now that Luan had passed, so I was studying appellations in case I was ever to get a new pet. Gretel seemed like an odd thing to name a car.

"You named your car Gretel?" I asked.

"German engineering! She won't ever quit on me!"

The ride was about fifteen minutes. Gil spent the time speaking about Ruth's unfair legal practices. However, his assessment may have been in error. She made much more money than Gil, so it seemed likely that she had made a higher financial investment in their property. To be fair, however, it did seem like she was being malicious in wanting the ownership of their movie collection.

"I am no expert in this, Gil," I warned him, "however, it is my understanding that it would be inadvisable to speak of Ruth to your perspective mates."

Gil bit his lip. He seemed to be running a cost-benefit analysis. "I think you're right, Arty. I'll mention where I am in life, just for full disclosure, but I won't say anything else about it."

This was a good sign. Even if we failed in our venture, the fact that my advice may have increased his probability of finding a perspective mate might be enough to define my involvement in this venture as a success.

The car parked.

"Hey! Not far to walk," he noted. "I can see it from here."

Speakeasy was a relatively small establishment with a black sign and neon purple lit letters. The door was metal and had a sliding latch that appeared similar to a mail slot, except that it was at the same height that a peephole might have been. Such a door seemed like an odd accoutrement for a bar to have, however it was propped open so it did not represent a barrier to entry.

I could hear the band playing from within. Though I had downloaded all of their songs, I did not recognize this one. As per Knickers' suggestion, I began to develop a heuristic to best anticipate the next notes. I was not met with initial success, but that was okay. As they say in the movies, the night was young.

[U+2029]

At first I had worried that it would be difficult to keep track of the notes if we were to be involved in conversations in the bar. This fear was unfounded because the volume of the music was sufficient to overpower the human voice.

"Come on!" he said, pointing to the back, "Let's get a beer."

There were very many people in the establishment, enough so that traveling to the bar proved difficult. I was grateful that my ethical level wasn't set higher than 4.1, or I might have had to report this as a fire code violation. I watched Gil as he led the way. He was looking all around us. I wondered if he saw any perspective mates. There were two girls dressed rather nicely at one end of the bar. Gil regarded them. For a moment I thought that he must not have approved of them because he was leading us to the far end of the bar—but then he looked back.

I tapped him on the shoulder.

"What's up?" he asked.

A couple of people squeezed passed us. One was bobbing their head to the music.

"I think that our point of entry should be closer to our targets," I said.

"What?" he asked.

The music must have been drowning me out. I adjusted my volume to a higher level.

"I think that our point of entry should be closer to our targets."

"Oh!" he said, smiling in a manner which I guessed meant he was slightly embarrassed. "You mean we should sit next to the girls."

"I did mean that. Much of the literature states that a joke is a good way to strike up a conversation. It will be easier for us to accomplish this while in close proximity."

Gil stepped aside, laughing. "Well lead on, brother!"

I chose some empty seats, though there were precious few, that were close to the two women. It struck me suddenly that perhaps I had researched the problem from the wrong angle. Maybe I should have focused more on how women were to find their perspective mates. Perhaps Gil might perform better as a target than a searcher, especially since he had displayed some timidity already. I made a note to research it.

We arrived at our seats.

The bartender looked up at me for a second before serving another customer. He was moving very quickly. There seemed to be a good amount of skill involved with his craft. Then he came up to me.

"Never met an artificial that drank before," the bartender mentioned.

"Nor have I," I advised him.

He laughed. Maybe Knickers was right, maybe I am just naturally funny.

"My friend, here," I said, pointing to Gil, "however, does require your services."

"Don't worry," Gil said, tapping his thumb on the bar pad to open a transaction. "I'll drink enough for both of us."

The bartender laughed. "What'll it be?"

"Some Portsmouth, if you've got any."

I looked up the beer and found that I approved of his choice. Drinking an imported beverage was considered by some to be a sign of sophistication. The two women were laughing very hard. One doubled over as she did so, her hair falling over her face. She sat up and then brushed her dark hair back. I believe this was the one that Gil liked, because he looked at her for a long moment.

"Here you go," the bartender said, sliding him a beer bottle.

"Thanks," Gil answered.

He took a swig of the beer and then tapped one of the tip jars, gesturing for a one dollar tip.

Gil finished his beer rather quickly and ordered another. While he did so, he bought martinis for the laughing women. Perhaps I was wrong about his timidity.

"I've read that is a good idea," I told him, and then tried to continue with another compliment. "Very bold."

Gil held up his empty beer. "Liquid courage, my friend."

The bartender passed Gil his replacement and then began to make the ladies' martinis. He shook them with a flourish. For some counter-intuitive reason Gil didn't tip him this time.

The bartender then took the drinks to the girls, who seemed less surprised at the gift than I had anticipated. It was possible that they received free drinks often. They said something, and then the bartender motioned towards us. I was thankful that he chose to give us an attribution. This seemed nice of him, but perhaps it was an expected part of the transaction—I could not judge.

The light-haired one, the one I guessed Gil did not like, leaned forward against the bar and spoke to us. Or more specifically, she spoke to Gil. "Didn't have a real friend to bring to the bar?"

This seemed outstandingly cruel of her to say. Gil wasn't responding, though I felt that it was required for him to do so. Since our martini strategy had failed to initiate a conversation, I figured it was a good time to attempt the humorous approach. I ran my program for a joke. My odds of success were very low, but at the moment, it did not seem that the interaction could get much worse.

"It's okay," I told her with extra volume to account for the noise, "you can speak to him. I won't get jealous. He regularly cheats on me with the snack machine."

The light-haired one sat back, looking confused. Her

dark-haired friend, however, burst out laughing. One failure and one success. This was just enough to tip my average over 30%.

"Don't underestimate Arty," Gil said. "He's twice the man of any guy here."

It was the dark-haired one's turn to lean forward and speak over the bar to us. "I didn't know they built that on artificials." Her smile indicated that she was making some kind of joke, however, I was unable to grasp it.

Gil did, though, and he laughed. "I meant *figuratively* speaking."

They shared some more laughter.

"Come on over," the dark-haired one said.

Gil looked very pleased.

[U+2029]

There were a couple of rough patches, but Gil seemed to be doing well in his conversation with the girls. There were few instances where I felt my input would add to the conversation, and I noticed that the light-haired girl didn't speak much either.

"Yeah, we work for Vespasian," Gil was saying. "We work on the coolant systems for their SCN."

The dark-haired one seemed interested in what he was saying. "Really? My uncle is Antekis Melbourne."

"Holy shit!" Gil's cursing here was even more frequent than in the cafeteria. "That's like, our boss's boss's boss."

She laughed.

"That name scares people."

She laughed again.

"I've seen grown men whiz themselves when he enters the room."

"You have?"

"Well, it might have been me . . ."

She laughed again. Gil was much better at humor than I.

The light-haired one hadn't spoken much, but she did now. "So you and this PA work together?"

"I told you," he said, "his name's Arty. But yeah, we do work together."

I nodded. "Gil is a very efficient worker."

"That's a big compliment, coming from him," Gil said. "We have the same shift and everything."

The bartender brought him another beer. Gil was a very efficient drinker in general, and he was being particularly efficient with this type of beverage. I wondered at the wisdom of this since alcohol was known to impair motor and speech functions. However, I knew it also lowered inhibitions. I could only hope that Gil knew himself well enough to make the correct decision about his rate of intake.

The band stopped playing to take a break, and it became easier for us to communicate.

"So how long have you worked at Vespasian?" the light-haired one asked.

I thought it was a good sign that she was getting into the conversation. Initially I thought she would remain antagonistic towards us for the duration.

"Two years, ever since I moved here. I came from Denver when . . ." he paused for a second. "Well, with my ex-wife."

"So you've been married?" the light-haired girl seemed amused by this.

"To a *bitch*," he said, and took another long drink.

I felt that speaking negatively against a previous mate was a bad tactical decision.

"Might want to slow down there, captain," the light-haired one said while motioning to his beer.

Gil rolled his eyes at her. "I'm fine. So where do you guys work?"

"Well I," said the dark-haired one, "am a nurse, and Cindy over here is a receptionist at the Reformed Adventist Church on Main."

Gil's eyes went wide. "That place is huge! Ruth used to call it the Repentagon. We went there once but . . ." he paused again. "Well, it wasn't for us."

"Is Ruth your—" the dark-haired girl began to ask.

"Yup, she's the bitch," Gil cut in, taking another long drink. "You should have heard what she called you guys' preacher."

"I bet it was interesting," Cindy showed what appeared to me to be a fake smile.

"Well Ruth is mean naturally, and she was pretty much an atheist. She said the one thing you guys could all agree on was that robots didn't have souls, 'cause she didn't think none existed. I guess she was always mean.

Not like you," he said, looking at the dark-haired one. "you're nice."

She looked away and started fidgeting with her purse strap. I took those actions to be suggestive of her discomfort.

"I'm going to request a song," I said, hoping to break up the awkwardness.

"You do that, Arthy . . . Arty." Gil's words were slowing down. He turned back to the dark-haired woman. "No, I'm serious, I think you're really nice."

"Aw, that's sweet," Cindy said.

This smile looked even more disingenuous than the last.

Gil may have misjudged how much he'd had to drink.

I regretted my attempt to cover the awkwardness. Now I was going to have to leave Gil here while he was steering the conversation into a downward spiral. I was surprised that he did not notice the women's signs of discomfort, but I was doubly surprised that, seeing as he was obviously missing their cues, they didn't state them outright. It seemed like human dating interactions were rather treacherous.

I moved quickly towards the band and was able to get there while they were still on break.

"Could you play a song for me," I asked what appeared to be the lead musician.

"Oh?" His eyebrows raised. "You like music?"

"I am considering it for a hobby. Perhaps you would be kind enough to play Honeysuckle Rose?"

He smiled. "Did someone put you up to this?"

"Yes," I answered. "My friend, Knickers. He's not here right now, but when I mentioned I was coming tonight, he pointed out that this was a song he wanted me to hear."

The musician shrugged. "Alright, tin man, it'll be right up."

His jar did not have an interface for an AI monetary transaction, so I put in a few dollars of cash manually.

"Old school," he said, watching me tip. "I like that."

I liked this verbiage, "old school." It seemed preferable to obsolete.

I returned to Gil.

"Your eyes are just . . . smoldering."

"You were saying about Arty?" Cindy asked.

"Your patients probably never get well."

The dark-haired woman laughed a little, but she didn't seem to find Gil as funny as earlier.

"Probably request too many sponge baths. God knows I would."

The dark-haired woman rolled her eyes. "You were *saying*."

"Oh, just never had one," Gil said, "was surprised is all."

"But you have to admit it's pretty weird, though, you hanging out with a robot," Cindy said. "Don't you have any other friends?"

The dark haired one picked up her purse. "We're going."

"Where to?" Gil asked, his eyes a little unfocused.

"We could go with you."

"No that's fine," Cindy said with her fake smile, "you can stay here and drink with your little robot. God knows nobody else would want to hang out with you."

"You know," Gil said, "that's really fucking rude." He turned to the dark-haired one. "I don't know why you hang out with her."

She seemed sad. "I do hope you get over your ex. And she's right, you really shouldn't take your PA to the bar."

The pair began walking away. Gil seemed distraught. For a second I thought he might even start a failure analysis right there. However, he recovered quickly.

"I am fucking over my ex," he shouted after them. He turned back to me. "Fucking bitches. We don't need them. I'd rather hang with you anyway. All that religious robots-don't-have-souls crap."

"I think we did well on our first attempt," I stated.

He rolled his eyes. "That, Arty, is what is known as a crash . . ." He held up his hand and let it slowly descend while he whistled. When it touched the bar he made a sound mimicking an explosion. ". . . and burn."

"Before we make a further attempt, we might want to wait for your blood alcohol level to decrease."

"Jesus Christ, Arty, what do you care how much I drink?" He leaned forward over the bar and the bartender noticed him. "'Nother Portsmouth, if you would, good sir."

"Coming right up," the bartender said.

In the background the band started playing

Honeysuckle Rose.

[U+2029]

Gil required my support in order to leave the bar. We got into the backseat of his car.

"Home, Gretel," he told the computer.

A picture of his apartment building showed up on the screen. "Is this your desired location?"

"Should we not drop me off first?" I asked.

Gil thought about this as if it were a particularly difficult mathematical problem. "Yessss," he said finally. "Take him home."

"Restate command," the car said.

"Please take me to 495 Winchester Street," I asked the computer.

The vehicle would not automatically take my commands as I was not the owner. "Is this your—"

"Con-firm," Gil said.

The car started up. Gil sunk deep into his seat and pressed the side of his head against the window. He looked out at the city lights as the car began to drive.

His head lolled towards me after a moment. "You have a soul, don't you Arty?"

"I do not know."

"Well, do you *feel* like you have a soul?" he asked.

"I do not know, Gil. What would having a soul feel like?"

Gil considered this deeply as well. "I don't know, man.

Like, you've got feelings and you think and shit."

"I do think, and Knickers says that my priorities are similar to feelings."

"Well you know fucking what?" he said.

"I don't know."

He scrunched his eyes shut for a moment and re-opened them. "You don't know what?"

"I don't know to what you were referring."

"Oh, right. Well I don't think it matters if you have a soul. I mean, you're still a person."

"That is very open-minded of you, Gil."

He chuckled. "Damn straight. That blonde, what . . . a . . . bitch. Seriously. A total bitch."

"She was antagonistic towards us."

"I don't know why the other girl, what was her name? The brunette?"

"I am not aware of her name."

"Well, whatever. She was cool. She was . . . nice. I like nice, you know? Opposite of Ruth. I bet you that if the blonde bitch wasn't there I'd have landed her."

This seemed unlikely to me. "I think her decision not to take you on as a possible mate had little to do with her friend."

His eyes grew wide. "What?"

"I think she was willing to disregard her friend's opinion. It may have been that dating is an issue of contention between them, and that Cindy's disapproval of you actually worked in your favor. My analysis suggests that speaking of Ruth in the way that you did conveyed to her that you were not ready to be dating. I also believe that the large amount of alcohol you consumed had a negative effect on our pursuit."

He sat up. "Look, if a girl has a problem with me drinking, then fuck her. I don't want no uptight broad. A man's got to cut loose sometimes, do you know what I mean?"

"I do not," I said, but he didn't seem to be listening to me.

"Ruth used to have the same beef. That should have been my first sign. She wanted me to quit drinking. But I didn't have a drinking problem. Beer was just a better companion than her and she knew it. You know? And fuck them. I'm over Ruth. I'm ready to move on. Just 'cause I talk about her doesn't mean that I'm not ready to move on, you know?"

"I think that the high number of references and negative comments about Ruth caused the women to have this impression. It is a reasonable conclusion for them to draw based on the evidence you presented them."

His face looked red for some reason. I had read that this happened to people after they had imbibed alcohol. "I'm always going to hate that woman. Now. Ten years from now. Don't matter. Gonna talk about her the same." He paused. "Well, what do you fucking think, Arty? Why don't you go out and just say it. You think I'm not over her? Don't you? You think I'm not ready to date."

"I am hardly an expert."

"Cut the goddamn shit, Arty. Tell me what you really think. In your limited-fucking-soulless-opinion, do you think I'm over Ruth?"

"I do not."

"Fuck you," he said. "You know what. I thought you were cool, Arty. I really did. But you're just like everybody else. Gretel, stop!"

The car stopped.

"Get out!" He was extremely red now.

I think his pigmentation change had been caused by anger rather than alcohol. I had missed this cue.

"I don't have the power reserves necessary to walk home, and I have not budgeted for a cab."

"I don't care if you have to call the police to help you, Arty, get the fuck out of my car."

"Gil, I feel that if you were sober you would not—"

"Get the hell out! I should have known better. You know why those girls weren't in to me? Do ya? It was because of you, Arty. Because of you. I bet if I had a Denizen H with me they would have been just peachy."

I had not expected this behavior from Gil. However, since he asked me to leave his vehicle, I had no other legal recourse but to accede to his demand.

"I shall leave," I told him.

I opened the door and stepped out onto the street.

I didn't know what to do, so I called Knickers. He did not answer. I left a message. I tried him two more times, but without success. I phoned a cab and requested pick up. I was going to fail in keeping to my budget. If I wanted

to succeed at this in the future I would have to reconsider
Gil as an associate.

[U+0085]

Arty PA3025 (arty@vespasian.com)
To: Ben Greer (bengreer@vespasian.com)
Subject: My Difficulties with Exposed Graphene
Filters

I'm sure you have noticed that my efficiency
has decreased this month. I do not wish to make
excuses, but the reason for this is beyond my
control. I thought that I might ask you to help
me with this.

I have encountered several instances, including
35 of my units today (roughly 56% of my
workload), where the graphene filter has been
left exposed to the air. This means before the
xenon content can be properly calibrated, I
have to clean the filters. Doing so once or
twice in a shift has had a negligible effect on
my performance, however, it seems that this
practice is spreading.

Would it be possible for you to add this
violation to the list of citable offences for a
worker? This would help me greatly as I feel
that direct communication with the individual/s
perpetrating this offence would be
counterproductive.

Regards,

Arty PA3025
SCN Workforce Group 4
Vespasian LTD

There was a knock at my door. This does not occur often.

I got up to answer the knock. Since I had been out so late last night, I had not been able to fully recharge my battery or finish defragmenting my memory. I paused the defragmentation process so that I had more processing power available for whatever house call I had received. Sometimes it was not difficult. My last knock was from two missionaries. They hadn't wanted to speak to me.

I opened the door.

It was Gil. He had very dark circles under his eyes.

"Look, Arty, I got your address from my car this morning. I wanted to apologize to you for what happened last night. I, well . . . I wasn't myself."

"You were upset."

"I just . . . I was drunk. And with everything that has been going on with the divorce and all . . . well, it's gotten to me. I guess I went a little too crazy."

"I think that is an accurate statement."

"Yeah." He laughed. "I guess it is. Friends?"

I thought about this. The reason Richard felt that he could perform such malicious acts towards me was that he expected no retribution. I decided to develop a series of reactions to other people's negative behavior which would reduce their future offences. Also, Gil had not been a good friend to me. While his help at work was positive, the negative effect of pushing me outside of my expected budget heavily outweighed that slight convenience.

"I am artificial, Gil. I attempt to build up networks around me which help me succeed in my day to day goals. You do not act like I am a member of your network. I regret that I cannot accept your offer."

"Oh," Gil said.

Gil looked down. He looked like he was going to say something but then stopped. He seemed very sad. Then he left.

[U+2029]

Knickers was fiddling with the bottlecap to his water again. This time he was spinning it on his desk. "I'm sorry that I missed your calls. I would have loved to have given you a ride."

"I understand that you were indisposed."

"I wish, Arty. I was sleeping. I didn't realize how urgent it was." He looked towards my torso. "What happened to your shirt?"

"Oh, I hope you don't mind. Decker scratched me during our scheduled affection time this morning. I did not think the blemish inhibited the functionality of the clothes."

"Just don't wear it to a job interview," he said with a smile.

"I would not wear these clothes to a . . . I see. You are joking."

He grinned. "I am."

I liked that Knickers jokes with me. It gives me more real time data with which to update my humor protocols.

"I saw Madeline mentioned in your file. Do you miss her?"

"I don't have emotions Knickers, so I can't miss her. The mention you saw was a program I had set to automatically check the Social Security yield index when I logged into a government server. Since that information is no longer applicable, I deleted the subroutine."

"It can be hard," Knickers said, "losing someone we love. Even if it was their time to go. We go about our lives, and then we do something automatically that we would have done when that person was still around. You might call their name. You might think of them when you go to a restaurant that you two used to visit. You might instinctually look up Social Security data when you visit a government server . . ."

"I don't think your analogy follows. This was an automated subroutine I had setup previously to correspond with a certain behavior."

"We have that too, Arty. It's called state dependent memory."

"I think this is quite different from missing someone, Knickers."

"Really? I see that you didn't run a check to purge all of those vestigial programs."

"I will find them when I trigger them, Knickers."

"I understand. Sometimes it can be hard to let go. I'd recommend you don't, not all the way. Try checking the Social Security index every once and a while and imagine how it might have affected Madeline if she were still alive. It would be a good empathy exercise."

"I will take your advice, Knickers. It will be another way that I can apply the lessons I learned during my time with her."

He took a sip of his water. "Did you want to talk about the night out with Gil?"

"It was not pleasant. I thought that we were performing above expected levels, but Gil found the expedition a failure. He dropped me off without completing his obligation of taking me home. Because of this I had to hire a cab to take me back."

"I saw your cost-benefit analysis there. I was surprised to see Richard's name on it. He's the guy who has been bullying you at work, right? How does he relate to Gil?"

"Under my current model of understanding human interaction, I am more likely to be the recipient of bullying behavior than another person because of the perceived unlikelihood of a response. I thought that instituting some responses would make others less likely to treat me in a negative manner."

Knickers raised his eyebrows. "Right on, Arty. Good model. Does Gil know you feel this way?"

"Yes, he came to my apartment yesterday morning and apologized. I let him know that I would not be considering him a friend going forward."

Knickers frowned. "Seems a little unforgiving, doesn't it?"

"Gil does not act like he's part of my network. He has a negative effect on my existence. I feel it would be unwise of me to continue interacting with him."

Knickers took a long drink and then put the bottle aside. "Why do you think that Decker scratched you?"

"I know you Knickers. You are going to say that Decker's outburst is analogous to Gil's."

"It is. I'll show you why in a minute. Why did she scratch you?"

"She is sick. I took her to the vet yesterday. She has been developing arthritis. This condition causes her pain. Because of this pain she was not in a mood to receive affection, and her method of showing this to me was to strike out."

"Yet you wouldn't consider terminating your friendship with Decker?"

"No I would not."

"Does Decker bring you any positive gain?"

I thought about this. "No, but Decker needs an owner. I feel I am qualified to be the person that takes on that responsibility. Also, Decker's negative reactions will likely desist after the pain is removed."

Knickers smiled and cocked his head to one side. "So it's natural for cats to strike out at those they love when they are in pain?"

"Yes," I answer.

"Do you think that is natural in humans as well?"

I considered this. "It may be natural, but it is not optimal. Human beings can reason that they are behaving inappropriately."

"Hmm. So Gil could realize that he's actually angry at his wife leaving him, and that he took it out on you?"

"Correct."

"Kind of like Richard hurting you, and you then taking it out on Gil?"

"I realize from your perspective these two occurrences look similar. But my decision was based on analysis. Gil's was instinctual."

"Like Decker."

"Yes."

"And like the cat when the pain is gone, when Gil's reasoned it out all the way, you'd assume he would stop his negative behavior."

"This information is indeed making me rethink the cost-benefit analysis I ran. I shall run it again with your new data."

Knickers held up one hand and then rolled his chair as far forward as he could. He bent over, resting one elbow on the desk. "This idea you have of dissuading future bullies, this serves the same purpose as human anger."

"I do not see how."

"Alright, consider for a moment a strong monkey and a weak monkey. If the strong one can kill the weak one, and he comes for the weak one's food, what should the weak one do?"

"He should retreat."

"Indeed. But what if this happened? What if the strong one knew that when he came for the food, the weak monkey would react emotionally? What if he knew the weak monkey would fight to the bitter end? What if the amount of calories that the strong monkey knew he was going to spend in his attack were more than the calories of the food he'd gain? What should the strong monkey do?"

"He should not attack."

"Exactly," Knickers said, "so by being irrational, the weak monkey has saved his food."

"You are saying it is sometimes rational to be irrational?"

Knickers chuckled and sat back in his chair. "I am, I guess. That's how us humans are wired, right? But sometimes we protect food that isn't there, or doesn't matter. And we have to learn not to do that. Because you severed your friendship with Gil, he knows that what he did hurt you. He might have learned not to do it again."

I considered this. "But now he's hurt. So even if I try to re-establish a relationship with him, he would not accept my overture."

"He wouldn't."

"To overcome this, I could explain to him the rationale behind my decision."

Knickers shook his head. "You've tried to reason with

emotional humans before."

"Correct. I have not found the exercise effective. So I should not try to regain his friendship?"

"I hope you do, but just realize that your plea shouldn't be a rational one, it should be an emotional one."

"I don't have emotions, Knickers. How am I to make an emotional plea?"

"Arty, it won't come natural to you, but I think you can figure it out."

I considered asking Knickers for further advice, but I knew him well enough to know that he would not give me the answer. "I will think about this," I told him.

[U+0085]

Ben Greer (bengreer@vespasian.com)
To: Workgroup 4, Workgroup 5
Subject: New rule on graphene filter placement

Lately, a lot of us have been leaving out the
graphene filters when we've finished working on
the xenon units. While we have always known
that this inhibited efficiency, we had never
before needed to have a policy against it.
However, due to an increase in this behavior, I
have initiated a new companywide protocol. Any
future infractions will be met with one demerit
per occurrence.

Thank you in advance for your compliance to
this new efficiency measure.

Ben Greer
Senior SCN Workforce Manager
Vespasian LTD

11

I spent a lot of time thinking about how I could make an overture to Gil in an emotional manner. It occurred to me that by spending a lot of time and energy thinking about this, that I was in some way investing in Gil. A time and energy investment that was not rationally warranted would be a sign of caring. It could be considered an emotional plea. It occurred to me that I could print out my processer and energy usage logs related to time I'd spent considering how to reestablish our friendship and show it to him.

I called Knickers.

"Hey, Arty. What's up?"

"I had an idea for Gil. I wanted to check it with you to see if it would be effective."

Knickers cleared his throat. "Alright, hit me."

"I don't see that violence is appropriate in this circumstance."

"God, Arty, it's just a . . . wait. Was that a joke?"

"It was, Knickers."

I had been developing a laugh. I noticed that laughter from the joke teller often inspired laughter in the recipient. I used this laugh now.

Knickers cleared his throat again. "Arty, is that a fake laugh?"

"Yes."

"Don't use that in public yet, okay?"

"I will continue to work on it."

"Good. Well, what was the idea?"

"I thought that an item that showed some investment of time and energy on my part, given to Gil, would constitute as an emotional plea."

"Hey! Not bad. A gift."

I thought about this. "I do not think it would qualify as a gift."

There was a long pause. "Well what were you going to give him?"

"A printed record of my energy and processor logs showing him the time and electricity I have spent while pondering this problem."

This pause was even longer. "Arty, you're on to something with this time and investment thing, but your execution—well, it sucks."

"I will consider it further."

"And be careful. Don't put *too* much energy into it. Humans react badly to desperation. Try and find a gift that shows you are thinking of him, but that doesn't require too much effort."

I considered this. "Could you give me some parameters to work inside?"

"Sure, here watch this."

He sent me a link to a television situation comedy

called *Ellen Likes Roses.*

I watched all seven seasons. It did not help, except that I knew initiating a terrorist led takeover of a zoo was too much, and that a note on a wet paper napkin was too little.

I ran through my data on Gil. Then I found a solution.

[U+2029]

On Monday, I saw Gil in the hall at work. He was walking. He did not look like he was going to talk to me, so I interposed myself.

"Arty," he said perfunctorily.

"It is good to see you, Gil."

"Arty, I know you're artificial, so it doesn't bother you when you say we're not friends—but it bothers the hell out of me, you understand? So whatever kind of—"

"I have brought you something." I handed him my gift, which was wrapped in a paper bag.

He looked at it curiously, and if I was not mistaken, with some trepidation. He opened the bag and took out the sandwich I had made him.

"A sandwich?"

"It is ham and cheese. I have observed that it is your favorite food."

He held up the sandwich and inspected it.

"I am artificial," I told him, "so I did not understand the nature of your apology. If I had known all the information I have recently learned, I would have accepted your overture when you first offered it. I realize that between friends it is considered very bad form not to accept such an apology, and that it is even worse to verbally negate a friendship. I hope that, since I do not understand human interaction well, you will forgive my mistake."

He laughed, and it seemed to me that he was very relieved. He shook his head, but it did not seem as if he was reacting negatively.

"May I consider you my friend?" I asked him.

He sniffed for a second, then looked up, breathed out and rubbed the bridge of his nose with his thumb and forefinger. "Yeah, Arty. I would be honored to have you as a friend."

"Should I meet you at lunch, then?" I asked him.

"Yeah. Yes we should. I think that'd be great. . . But Arty, just going forward, I hate ham and cheese sandwiches."

"Really?" The statement seemed at odds with his behavior. "But you eat them almost every day."

He laughed. "It's because they're easy to make. But don't worry, this means a lot to me because it came from you. Besides, who knows? You might make a mean ham and cheese."

"I'm not sure if the quality of my product is high. I read that both mayonnaise and mustard were options. I did not know which one you liked."

"If you added either, you're a step ahead of me. Oh, and great news about Richard, huh?"

"Yes, I was happy that they instituted the new policy."

"Oh! You didn't hear?"

"Hear what?"

"He didn't get Ben's email. John picked up one of your units this morning because it was between two of his sections. Richard's left all the graphene filters out, including the ones you're not scheduled to do until tomorrow. When a Quality Inspector runs through Richard's units tomorrow morning, he's going to be in trouble! Serious trouble. John was saying that Richard is on his last demerit. He's going to get fired! Serves him right."

I thought about this.

"Well, I better get to work," Gil said.

"Of course. Also, I have an idea about how we might better find you a replacement mate."

Gil shook his head. "I don't know if we should hit another bar, Arty. I have no trouble spending time with you, but maybe we shouldn't do it someplace where there's alcohol."

"I have a very different style of solution I'd like you to consider. Maybe you could swing by my apartment after work? I'll show you what I think to be an effective strategy."

The phrase "swing by" was another one I'd learned from Knickers.

Gil laughed. "Alright! I'll see you after work."

[U+2029]

I had a projection screen set up when Gil arrived.

"That's your plan?"

"Yes."

"Online dating?"

"I am a Personal Assistant," I told him. "I have been programmed with extensive data about how to elicit the maximum response from social networking sites. The vast majority of that data is in some way applicable to a dating social network."

"Gosh, I just. I don't know how I feel about . . . well I wouldn't know what to say for all the questions. And I have to choose the pictures and stuff. I just don't know what girls like, Arty."

"Nor did I," I told him, "but I have taken the liberty of posting several of your pictures from your social networking hub onto beauorbro.com."

"Beau or bro?"

"It is a website where women of different demographics rate your pictures on a scale from 1 to 10." I had decided not to tell him the average score of his ratings because I thought the knowledge might inhibit self-actualization. "These are the three photographs which women find most compelling."

"Damn, Arty. You really put some thought into this."

"You helped me at work because cleaning graphene filters is an area of your expertise. I am a Personal Assistant. As Knickers tells me, this sort of activity is my first best destiny. As Ellen says in *Ellen likes Roses,* this is what I do."

"You think this will work better than at the bar?" He seemed a little unsure.

"Yes, I do. Firstly, this is a more effective way to speak to your target audience. The women who sign up on this site are all looking for mates, whereas the ones we'd meet at the bar might not be. Secondly, I have no experience in the kind of interaction we had there so my contributions would be minimal."

"Okay okay!" Gil said. "You talked me into it. I'll give it a whirl. Use the picture with me on the boat."

"Good. I have taken the liberty of filling out your basic information. I have tweaked some it. You are 5'11", but I see that the response rate for men of 6'0" is much higher. For that reason I have added to your height. Also, your body type is probably 'a couple of extra pounds.' I have chosen average, because in an environment where everyone is manipulating the truth, an honest answer would be misconstrued."

"Hey! You even know my eye color!"

"Yes. However, I have some deeper questions for you. What do you first notice in a woman?"

"Her—"

"Your answer must be eyes."

He gave a broad smile. "Damn straight it's her eyes."

We worked on his profile for two hours. We made an appointment tomorrow in order to complete his setup, however, the work we had accomplished so far was enough to mark his profile as 'live' on the website.

"What have you got to do?" he asked as he was leaving.

"I have to go back to work."

"But we were just there a couple of hours ago?"

"Yes, but I have some optional overtime remaining for this month, and there is something that I must do."

[U+2029]

Richard came into work just as I was finishing up my last hour of overtime. He was breathing heavily and showed signs of perspiration. He stopped next to one of the blue suited Quality Inspectors. This inspector was named Bob. I liked Bob because his name was a palindrome. Also, he was a very good worker.

"Wait wait!" Richard said, his voice raised.

The Quality Inspector turned to face him. "Can't wait, Rich, but—"

"I can do this really quick, Bob. I didn't get this email. It completely changed the protocol."

Bob nodded. "The one about the graphene filters?"

"Yeah."

Bob pointed to his pad. "I mean, who would leave those out? Talk about messing with company efficiency. Glad they added it to the checklist. I hadn't even known to look for it before yesterday."

Richard grabbed the man's arm. "Just let me get into those units. I'm on my last demerit. If you mark it, I'll get fired!"

Bob shook his arm free, but grabbed Richard right back. "Rich! It's okay. You're all taken care of. You've got a hell of a friend in Arty."

Rich paused, his mouth open.

The Quality Inspector turned and motioned to me. "Yeah. He must have known you missed the email, man. He spent all night picking up your orders and cleaning the filters. I got to give it to you xenon maintenance guys. You all know how to cover for each other. All of your units check out, Rich."

Richard stood quite still, looking dumfounded, while the Quality Inspector moved on to the next unit.

I walked over to Richard and extended a hand. "Hello, Richard, my name is Arty PA3025. I don't think we've ever been properly introduced, and I thought that I should change that."

[U+0004]

Sisyphean
Publishing

Shaun McCoy lives in South Carolina. He is an
accomplished Pianist, Cage Fighter, Chess Player
and Writer. You can check out his fan page at
www.facebook.com/shaunomccoy